Town Teddy & Country Bear

Go Global

Town Teddy & Country Bear
Go Global

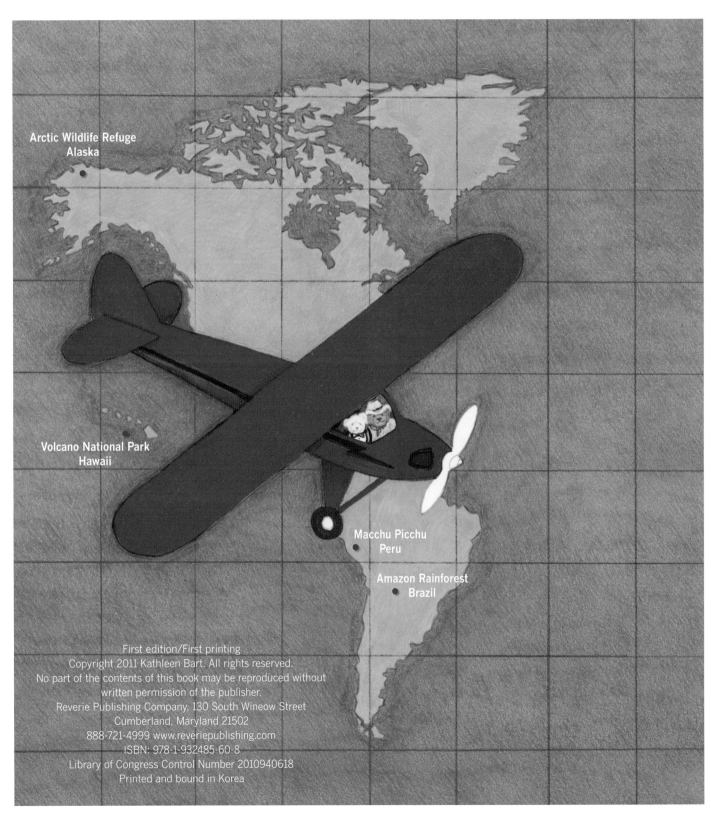

Arctic Wildlife Refuge
Alaska

Volcano National Park
Hawaii

Macchu Picchu
Peru

Amazon Rainforest
Brazil

First edition/First printing
Copyright 2011 Kathleen Bart. All rights reserved.
No part of the contents of this book may be reproduced without
written permission of the publisher.
Reverie Publishing Company, 130 South Wineow Street
Cumberland, Maryland 21502
888-721-4999 www.reveriepublishing.com
ISBN: 978-1-932485-60-8
Library of Congress Control Number 2010940618
Printed and bound in Korea

Written and Illustrated by
Kathleen Bart

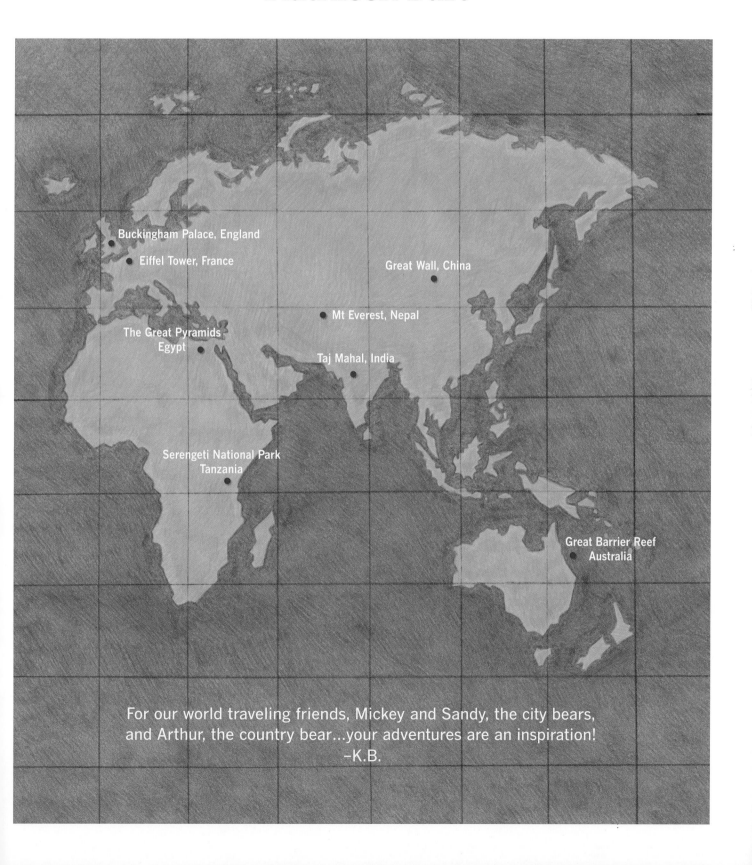

Buckingham Palace, England

Eiffel Tower, France

Great Wall, China

Mt Everest, Nepal

The Great Pyramids
Egypt

Taj Mahal, India

Serengeti National Park
Tanzania

Great Barrier Reef
Australia

For our world traveling friends, Mickey and Sandy, the city bears,
and Arthur, the country bear...your adventures are an inspiration!
–K.B.

"I want to see the wonders of the world!" thought Bandanna Bear. "The earth has so many natural habitats to explore. Tropical reefs to snorkel. Arctic ice to dog sled. Rainforest treetops to zip line. I think I'll trek the globe with my city cousin, Tuxedo Teddy."

"I want to tour the wonders of the world," mused Tuxedo Teddy. "The earth has so many historic sites to see. Ancient ruins to explore. Fabulous architecture to admire. Famous landmarks to visit. I think I'll take a world tour with my country cousin, Bandanna Bear!"

The cousins stayed up all night packing for their trip. Bandanna stuffed his nature journal into his backpack. "I can't wait to explore the world's natural wonders."

Tuxedo packed his passport into his luggage. "I can't wait to tour the cultural wonders of the world."

The traveling teddies climbed aboard their plane and took to the sky with a cheer. "Yee Haa!" "Fabulous!"

The cousins' first stop was South America. They were glad to escape the cold winter weather back home. They landed in the mountain peaks of Peru to tour the lost city of Machu Picchu.

"I had no idea the Inca Trail was so exhausting!" Tuxedo whined as he climbed the steep steps to the ancient ruins. Bandanna urged him on. "Think how much you'll enjoy the view when you've worked for it."

As they climbed through the clouds, Machu Picchu appeared between the mountain peaks. Tuxedo was impressed with the sight of the forgotten paradise. "This was definitely worth the climb!"

The Lost City of Machu Picchu

Peru

These ancient ruins were at the top of my list of sites to see! The Incas, the native people of Peru, built Machu Picchu on the peaks of the Andes Mountains more than 500 years ago. This well-planned city is proof of their advanced building and farming skills.

Experts think this mystical city may have been a sun-worship site or a retreat for Incan rulers. The Incas eventually abandoned this paradise. The city remained "lost" for centuries until an archeologist uncovered it in 1911.

—Tuxedo Teddy

Bandanna admired the leaves and trees of the Amazon Rainforest from their plane. "Let's zip line through the treetops!"

The cousins climbed to the top of the tree canopy. "I feel like I'm in a sauna at the spa!" Tuxedo gasped, mopping the sweat from his brow.

Bandanna clipped himself to the zip line, jumped off the platform and soared towards the next tree. "Yee Haa! I'm Tarzan, king of the jungle!"

Tuxedo cautiously stepped off the platform. He panicked when he picked up speed. "I can't slow down!" he shrieked. Bandanna caught him just before he slammed to a stop.

The Amazon Rainforest

Brazil

The Amazon Rainforest is the largest rainforest in the world! Its oxygen-producing trees and plants provide fresh air for the planet to breathe. Every day, trees are cut down to make paper and lumber, and to clear the land for people's growing needs. If too many trees are cut, the earth's climate is harmed. The loss of trees also means the loss of homes for many rainforest animals.

I'll be sure to use recycled paper from now on. Save paper and save a tree!

—Bandanna Bear

The cousins crossed the Atlantic Ocean to the
continent of Europe. They arrived in London
just in time to see the Changing of the Guard
at Buckingham Palace. Chilly rain set a somber
mood. "Good thing I remembered my "'brolly',"
Tuxedo said, feeling very British.

Buckingham Palace

London, England

The Changing of the Guard ceremony has been a tradition at Buckingham Palace ever since Queen Victoria resided there in 1837. The old guard stands at attention in front of the palace. A trumpet blares, announcing the arrival of the new guard as they march in. Once the palace keys are handed over, the new guard is officially on duty.

You can tell if the Queen is home by looking at the flagpole at the top of the palace. If the flag is raised, the Queen is in!

—Tuxedo Teddy

Huddled under Tuxedo's umbrella, the bears waited for the ceremony to begin. The guards stood still as toy soldiers. Bandanna elbowed Tuxedo. "Why are they so serious?"

"Protecting the Queen and her palace is an honor," Tuxedo whispered.

The Changing of the Guard was full of fanfare. Once the new guard took their posts, a marching band paraded by the palace. Bandanna marched right along, knees lifted and arms swinging.

Paris was their second stop in Europe. "Ahh, there's nothing like Paris in the springtime," Tuxedo sighed as they strolled its wide boulevards. He swooned when he glimpsed the Eiffel Tower shimmering above the skyline. It twinkled as if it were decorated with diamonds. "Ooh la la! No wonder they call Paris 'The City of Light'!"

Bandanna couldn't resist dashing through the brightly lit fountains shouting, "Vive La France!"

Tuxedo shook his head. "I hoped we'd make a splash in Paris, but this isn't what I had in mind."

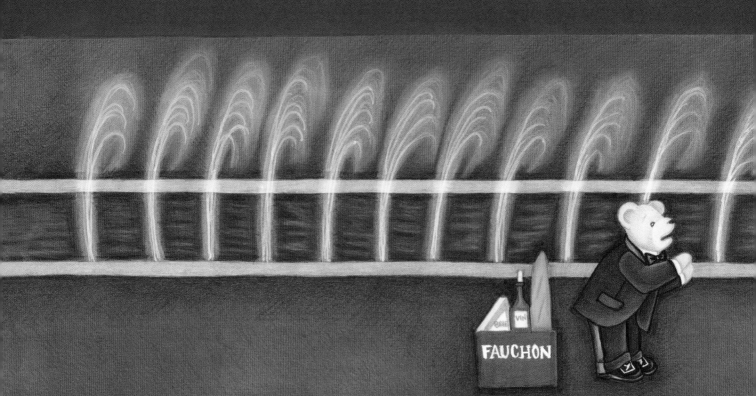

The Eiffel Tower

Paris, France

Gustave Eiffel created this famous tower for the Paris World's Fair in 1889. I was shocked to learn that the Parisians thought the Eiffel Tower was unattractive when it was first built. In fact, it was almost torn down!

Apparently, Monsieur Eiffel's creation was avante garde... ahead of its time! Today the Eiffel Tower is the most visited monument in the world. It's considered the symbol of Paris, and an icon of taste and style.

—Tuxedo Teddy

Crossing the Mediterranean Sea, the cousins touched down in Cairo, in search of ancient wonders. "Fabulous! I've always wanted to see Egypt. It's the site of one of the oldest civilizations in the world," Tuxedo explained.

The Great Pyramids appeared across the desert though waves of hazy heat. "Let's hitch a ride with the caravan. It's headed straight for the pyramids," Bandanna suggested. He climbed aboard a camel and dug his heels into its hump. "Yee Haa! Ride 'em cowboy!"

Tuxedo felt like he was on top of a moving mountain of fur. "I'm falling!" he cried as he started to slide off the camel's backside. Bandanna grabbed him just before he slid into the scorching sand.

The Great Pyramids

Egypt

In ancient Egypt, Pharaohs were believed to be gods who would live again after death. The Pyramids were built as tombs for the Pharaohs and all their treasures. They were buried with their wealth so they could live it up in the afterlife!

How the pyramids were built without modern tools remains a mystery. Still standing after 5,000 years, they are one of the last remaining Wonders of the Ancient World.

—Tuxedo Teddy

The teddies reached Serengeti National Park just as the sun was rising. A hot-air balloon was waiting to whisk them off on an African safari.

Bandanna eagerly took the controls. "We'll see the animals from the sky!" With a hiss of hot air, the balloon began to float. Drifting like a cloud, the cousins gazed at the animals below. Bandanna brought the balloon down for a closer look and almost snagged it on a thorny tree. Tuxedo clung to the tipping basket for dear life. "Are you sure you're capable of flying this contraption?"

Serengeti National Park
Tanzania

"Safari" is the Swahili word for "journey." A safari is a journey to observe wildlife, but that wasn't always the case.

I was sad to learn that in the past, a safari was really a hunting trip. Elephants and rhinos were hunted for their tusks. Zebras and leopards were hunted for their fur. As a result, these animals are now very few in number.

Thankfully, in recent years land has been set aside to create national parks and wildlife reserves where endangered animals are now protected. I'm so glad that endangered animals have a place where they're safe!

—Bandanna Bear

The teddies touched down in exotic India to tour the Taj Mahal. "I've always wanted to see this magnificent monument," Tuxedo sighed. "It's the Jewel of India."

Relaxing in the gardens, they gazed at the image of the Taj Mahal mirrored in the reflecting pool. Bandanna sat in a yoga pose called "lotus." "Did you know that yoga began right here in India? Check it out...I can bend like a gummy bear!"

Tuxedo tried twisting his legs into "lotus," but they got stuck in pretzel position. "I guess I'm not meant to be a yoga bear!"

The Taj Mahal

India

Emperor Shah Jahan built the Taj Mahal in memory of his wife, Mumtaz Mahal. He hired 20,000 workers to build a final resting place worthy of his beloved queen. It took twenty years to create a monument as grand as his love for his wife. Built of fine white marble and decorated with precious jewels, it is considered a masterpiece of architecture. I was enchanted by the Taj Mahal...and its romantic history!

—Tuxedo Teddy

Cruising high over the Himalayan Mountains, the bears flew to Katmandu. They hoped to be one of the few to reach the peak of Mount Everest. "I've always dreamed of climbing the tallest mountain on earth," Bandanna sighed.

The cousins loaded their supplies on the back of a yak and began the challenging climb. Snow swirled in their eyes. A biting wind stung their faces. The thin air was hard to breathe.

When the bears finally reached the summit, they were in awe of the view. "I feel like I'm on the top of the world!" Tuxedo gasped.

"That's because we are!" Bandanna beamed.

Mount Everest

Nepal, Tibet

Mount Everest is the tallest peak in the world, and the most challenging to climb. Climbers face avalanches, sudden snowstorms and blizzard-like winds. They often need oxygen tanks to breathe in the high altitude. Few climbers reach the summit.

The people of Nepal call Mt. Everest "Sagarmatha," meaning "Goddess of the Sky." Many climbers seek the mountain's blessing by flying prayer flags before beginning their trek to the summit. They believe that prayers are released to the spirits when the flags flap in the wind.

—Bandanna Bear

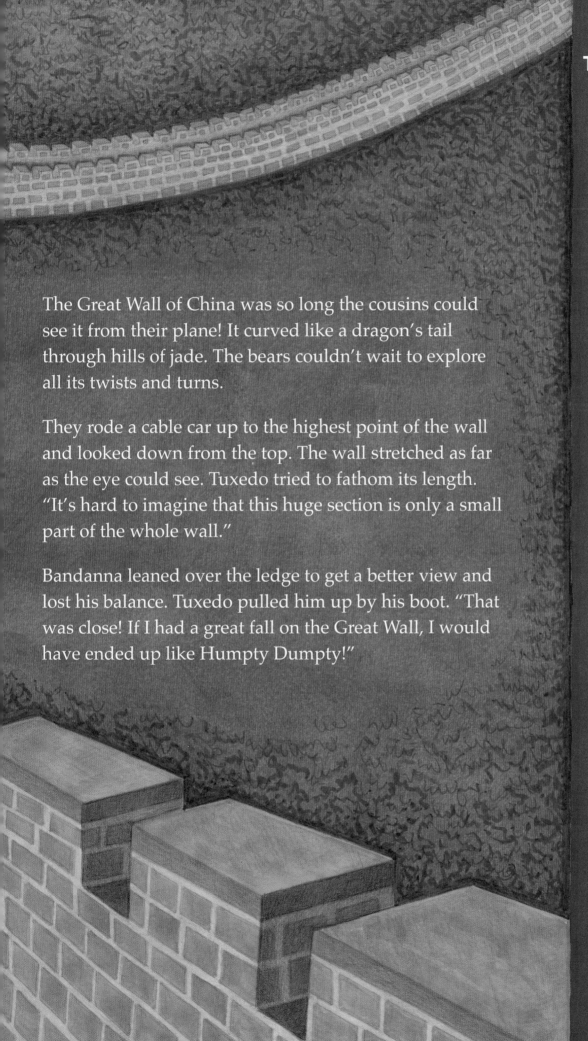

The Great Wall of China was so long the cousins could see it from their plane! It curved like a dragon's tail through hills of jade. The bears couldn't wait to explore all its twists and turns.

They rode a cable car up to the highest point of the wall and looked down from the top. The wall stretched as far as the eye could see. Tuxedo tried to fathom its length. "It's hard to imagine that this huge section is only a small part of the whole wall."

Bandanna leaned over the ledge to get a better view and lost his balance. Tuxedo pulled him up by his boot. "That was close! If I had a great fall on the Great Wall, I would have ended up like Humpty Dumpty!"

The Great Wall

China

The Great Wall of China is the largest man-made monument ever built. Emperors of ancient dynasties began building the wall more than 2,000 years ago. Millions of workers contributed to the construction of this legendary landmark.

The Great Wall is more than 4,000 miles long ... that's longer than the U.S.A. from coast to coast. If you walked ten miles a day, it would still take more than a year to walk the whole wall!

—Tuxedo Teddy

The bears flew over the Equator and "down under" to the continent of Australia. They boarded a boat headed for The Great Barrier Reef. When they reached the reef, Bandanna strapped on his snorkel mask and somersaulted into the sea. Floating face down, he could see tropical fish playing peek-a-boo in the colorful coral.

Tuxedo joined his cousin with a clumsy splash…and found himself snout to snout with a hungry shark. Frozen with fear, he could only bubble, "Help!" Bandanna rushed to the rescue and pulled him to safety. "I nearly became a shark's supper!" Tuxedo sputtered.

Great Barrier Reef

Australia

I discovered that the Great Barrier Reef is the largest coral reef in the world. Coral looks like plants or rocks but the living polyps are actually tiny animals. The reef provides shelter for fish and other sea life.

This delicate ecosystem is being harmed by pollution. When the reef is damaged, the rest of the sea life suffers, too. We need to be more careful and protect the coral reefs!

—Bandanna Bear

Gliding on a gentle breeze, the cousins cruised over the Pacific Ocean. As they hovered over the Hawaiian Islands, Bandanna pointed to a huge volcano on the Big Island. "There's Kilauea, the most active volcano on earth!"

Diving down to get a closer view, they gazed into the simmering crater. Red-hot lava bubbled like witch's brew. Puffs of smoke signaled trouble. "It's about to erupt!" Tuxedo warned. They sped away just as a fountain of fiery lava spewed into the sky.

"Yee Haa, nature's fireworks!" Bandanna cheered.

Volcanoes National Park

Hawaii

Lava is hot molten rock from deep inside the earth. When lava erupts through a volcano, it destroys everything in its fiery path.

Hawaiian mythology offers a less-scientific explanation. Legend says that Pele, the moody goddess who resides at Kilauea, is to blame for the eruptions. Islanders leave offerings to please her and keep her calm. If she gets angry, she'll have a meltdown and cause Kilauea to erupt. Talk about a hot temper!

—Bandanna Bear

The cousins traveled from the hot tropics to the icy Arctic. A dogsled was waiting to take them to watch polar bears swimming in the sea. "C ... c... can't we see polar bears from a c...c...cruise ship?" Tuxedo inquired through chattering teeth.

"Mush!" Bandanna shouted in reply. The dogs sprang into action, pulling the sled across the thin ice. Suddenly, a snapping sound filled the air. The sled tilted back into a crack, nearly tossing Bandanna into the frigid water. "Grab my paw!" Tuxedo yelled, as he steered the sled back onto solid ice.

Arctic National Wildlife Refuge

Alaska, USA

Polar bears are marine mammals. They spend most of their time hunting on sea ice in the Arctic Ocean. Unfortunately, climate change and warming temperatures are melting the arctic ice. If there isn't enough ice, the polar bears won't be able to hunt and get enough food to eat. We need to slow down climate change and save the polar bears!

—Bandanna Bear

The traveling teddies exchanged bear hugs before boarding their plane for home. They had shared so many amazing experiences on their world tour. Bandanna browsed through his nature journal and smiled. "We explored the earth's environments from the sky, the sea and the land!"

Tuxedo studied the stamps in his passport with pride. "We toured historic sites in all seven continents!"

The teddies' tour was over but their memories would last a lifetime. Tuxedo Teddy and Bandanna Bear headed home, feeling a little closer to the world and all its wonders.